W9-BKF-512

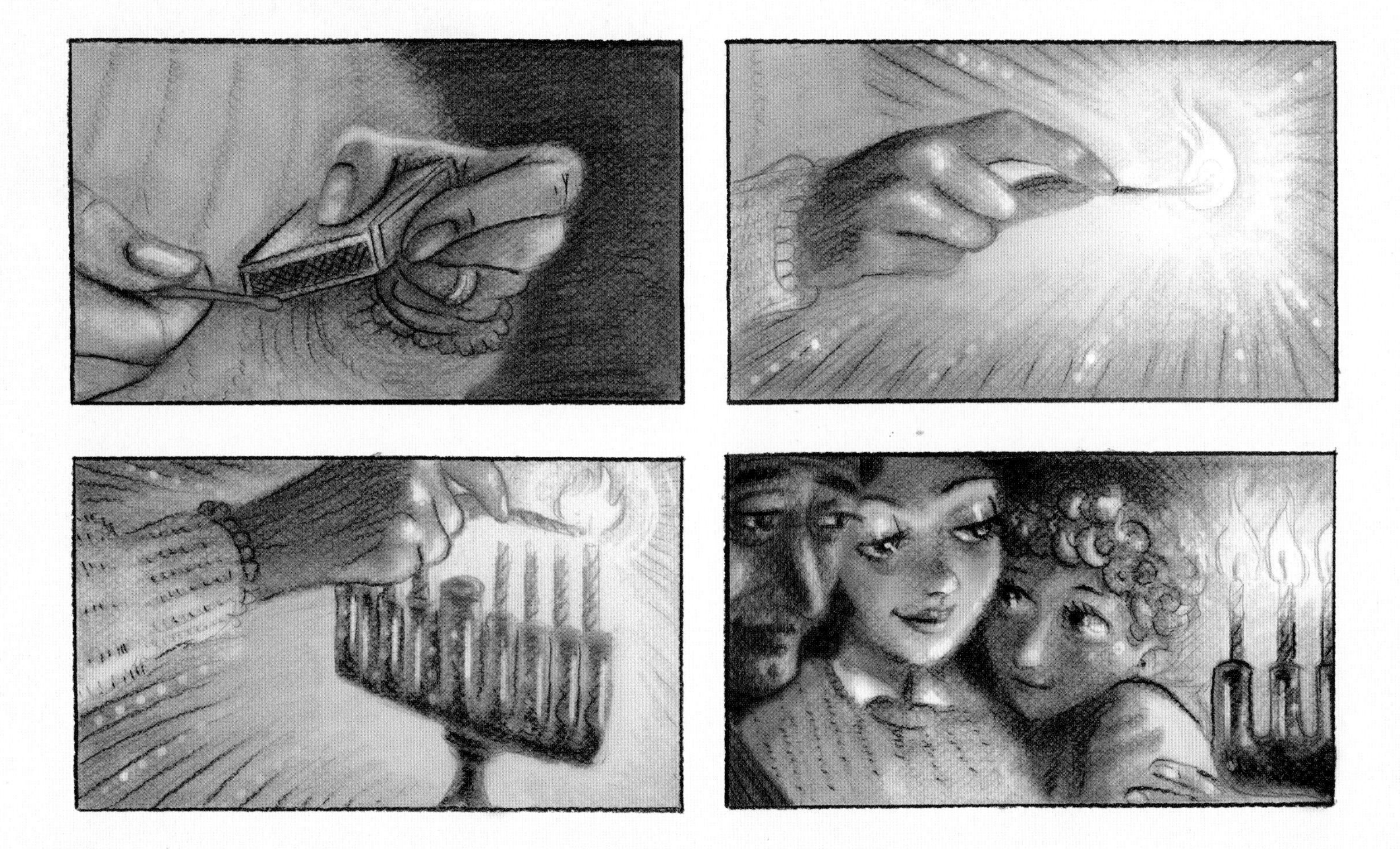

Oskar's mother and father believed in the power of blessings.

So did Oskar . . .

. . . until the Night of Broken Glass.

His parents put him on a ship to America. He had nothing but an address and a photo of a woman he didn't know—

"It's your Aunt Esther."

—and his father's last words to him:

"Oskar, even in bad times, people can be good. You have to look for the blessings."

Oskar and the Eight Blessings

RICHARD SIMON and TANYA SIMON

Illustrated by MARK SIEGEL

ROARING BROOK PRESS

New York

OSKAR arrived in New York on the seventh day of Hanukkah. It was also Christmas Eve.

He knew his Aunt Esther would be lighting the menorah at sunset. To reach her before the sun went down Oskar would have to walk over a hundred blocks on the avenue called Broadway.

The city was terribly big, Oskar was terribly small,
and Broadway stretched before him like a river.

Oskar was already tired, hungry, and cold.
His father's last words to him felt very far away.

After a few blocks, he looked up to see a woman
feeding pigeons.

She offered him a piece of a stale roll so he could feed them, too.

Oskar wanted to feed the birds, but he was too hungry not to swallow the morsel himself.

The woman reached inside her coat
and gave him a small loaf of bread.

It was warm and fresh. It gave him the
strength to keep walking.

Coca-Cola
ENTRANCE
ACTION COMICS
LIFE

He saw a newsstand full of comics.

One showed a strongman in a cape, doing amazing things.

He stopped bullets. He stopped trains.

The newsstand man held out his hand. Oskar didn't have money, so he gave back the comic book.

The man called to him.

COLLIERS
LIFE
SCIENCE TODAY
BLACK MASK

"Keep it, kid. Merry Christmas."

Oskar clutched
his gift, his super
man, and he
heard his father's
words . . .

. . . You have to look for the blessings.

Oskar kept walking. He stopped when he heard music coming from a little alley, where a big man was humming a jazzy tune. The man whistled to Oskar.

Oskar whistled back!

They made a tune as fast and light as the snowflakes falling around them.

It was Oskar's first conversation in America.

At the corner of a park, boys were having a snowball fight.

One boy slipped. Oskar leapt and caught him, just as the super man would have done.

The boy was laughing and that made Oskar laugh. But when he looked at Oskar's cold hands, he stopped laughing. He took off his mittens.

Oskar put them on and felt the boy's warmth. He had something to give the boy, too.

A few blocks later a tall lady in a big coat walked out of a building.
A policeman shouted, “Stand aside!”

Oskar stopped short.

“Oh, Thomas, he’s just a child,” the lady said to the policeman.
“Let him pass.” She winked at Oskar.

The policeman moved out of Oskar's path.

"Yes, Mrs. Roosevelt."

Mrs. Roosevelt!

The sun was setting and Oskar began to run. He had to get to Aunt Esther's before she lit the *shamash*.

Running, he stumbled, and fell.

A hand reached down . . .

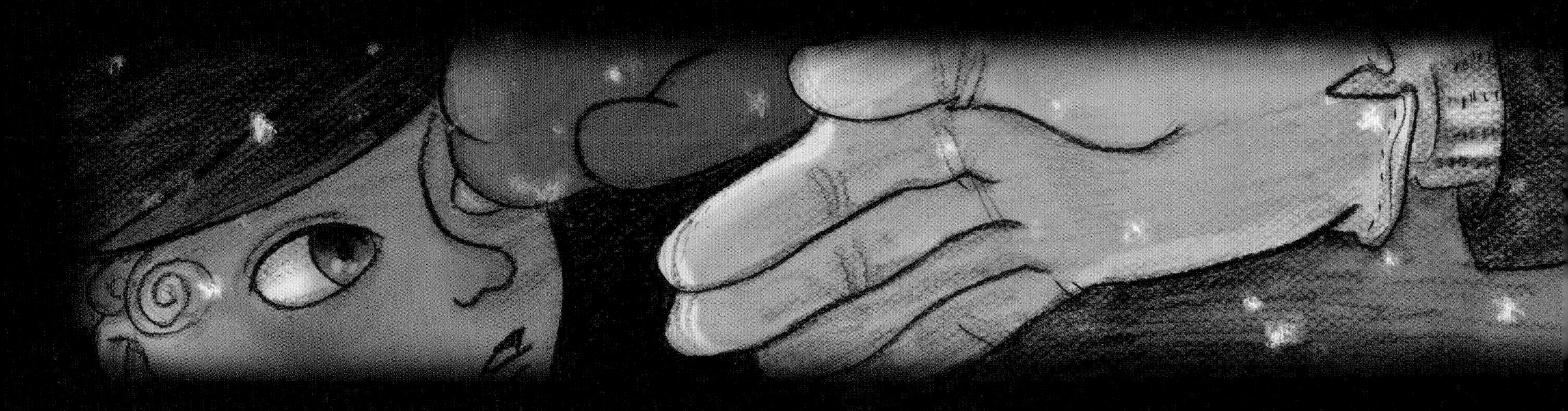

. . . and pulled him up. “Back on your feet, son.”

His father was right. *People can be good.*

He turned the corner and ran down the street, looking for her house.

He ran past a woman humming a *nigundl*.

Suddenly he heard a name.

“Benjamin?”

It wasn't his name. It was his father's, and it washed over him.

She had a dimpled smile just like his.

"That's Papa," he said, "I'm—"

"Oskar!" whispered Aunt Esther.

Author's Note

When I was ten, my grandfather told me the story of the three rabbis who traveled from our family's village in Lithuania to New York in 1938 to ask him, the eldest son of the eldest son of their *Rebbe,* to return with them and take his rightful place as the new *Rebbe.* He politely declined. He stayed in Brooklyn and drove a New York City bus the rest of his working life. The rabbis returned home and perished in the Holocaust.

I wondered about the three rabbis. What if they had stayed in New York? Why didn't they stay? Didn't they know what would happen? Did they know and go back anyway? I wondered about all the people whose lives were extinguished by the Holocaust. As a Jewish boy who had "survived" it by managing to be born half a generation after it, I imagined all the daring and sly ways I would have escaped the Nazis, and how I would have outwitted them all—especially Hitler, who always played the role of the devil in my imagination. Those fantasies were my consolation in the face of a horror I couldn't comprehend, even as I couldn't stop thinking about it.

Oskar is the fruit of those fantasies—the idea that what needed to be saved was not just lives but hope.

I grew up on Long Island, close enough to Manhattan to visit, and just far enough for each visit to be special, a trip to a land where wonder meets history. New York City for me has always been history itself, a place where you can feel yourself in history just by walking down the street. That's why Oskar escapes the nightmare of Nazi Germany and finds himself a part of history, not just because of what he lived through, but also because of what he can now hope to become.

In 1938, the year the rabbis came to find my grandfather, the year of *Kristallnacht*, the year where this story is set, the last night of Hanukkah was also Christmas Eve. That morning, First Lady Eleanor Roosevelt, a fixture of humanist intent in a world seemingly gone mad, left New York City to fly back to Washington, D.C. The night before, Count Basie and a host of other legends performed at Carnegie Hall in the groundbreaking "From Spirituals to Swing" concert. It was also the year Superman was born.

Oskar's particular blessings are blessings that only a major cosmopolitan city can bestow on a refugee. They represent all our potential to survive and even thrive in the face of great loss. In the words of Victor Frankl, "Everything can be taken from a man but one thing: the last of human freedoms—to choose one's attitude in any given set of circumstances, to choose one's own way." Oskar has lost everything, but from his despair he awakens to his freedom: the choice to see the good in his new world. I like to think that this orientation of optimism is the key to our survival, as individuals and as a species. It is how we, as American Jews, have made a place for ourselves beyond the shadow of darkness that tried to destroy us.

Richard Simon
New York, 2014

shamash [shuh-MAHSH]: The ninth candle on a Hanukkah menorah, usually standing above or below the other eight. It is the "servant" or "helper" candle, because it is lit first and then used to light all the others.

nigundl [NEE-g'n-d'l]: A *nigun* is a kind of Jewish religious music, a wordless melody usually sung with "nonsense" syllables (yi-di-di-di, ay-ay-ay . . .). *Nigundl* is an affectionate way of saying it, a "little nigun."

Kristallnacht [kris-TAHL-nakht]: On November 9, 1938, the Nazi governments of Germany and Austria authorized a *pogrom*—a violent mob attack on people from a particular ethnic group—against all Jews, all synagogues, and all businesses owned by Jewish people in both countries. In two days, over a thousand synagogues were burned down, thousands of Jewish-owned businesses destroyed, and more than 30,000 Jews were thrown into concentration camps. Also called Pogrom Night, and Night of Broken Glass, it was the first wide-scale step in what was called the Final Solution: the Nazi plan to murder all the Jews of Europe.

In Oskar's Footsteps

Trinity Church

Union Square

Herald Square

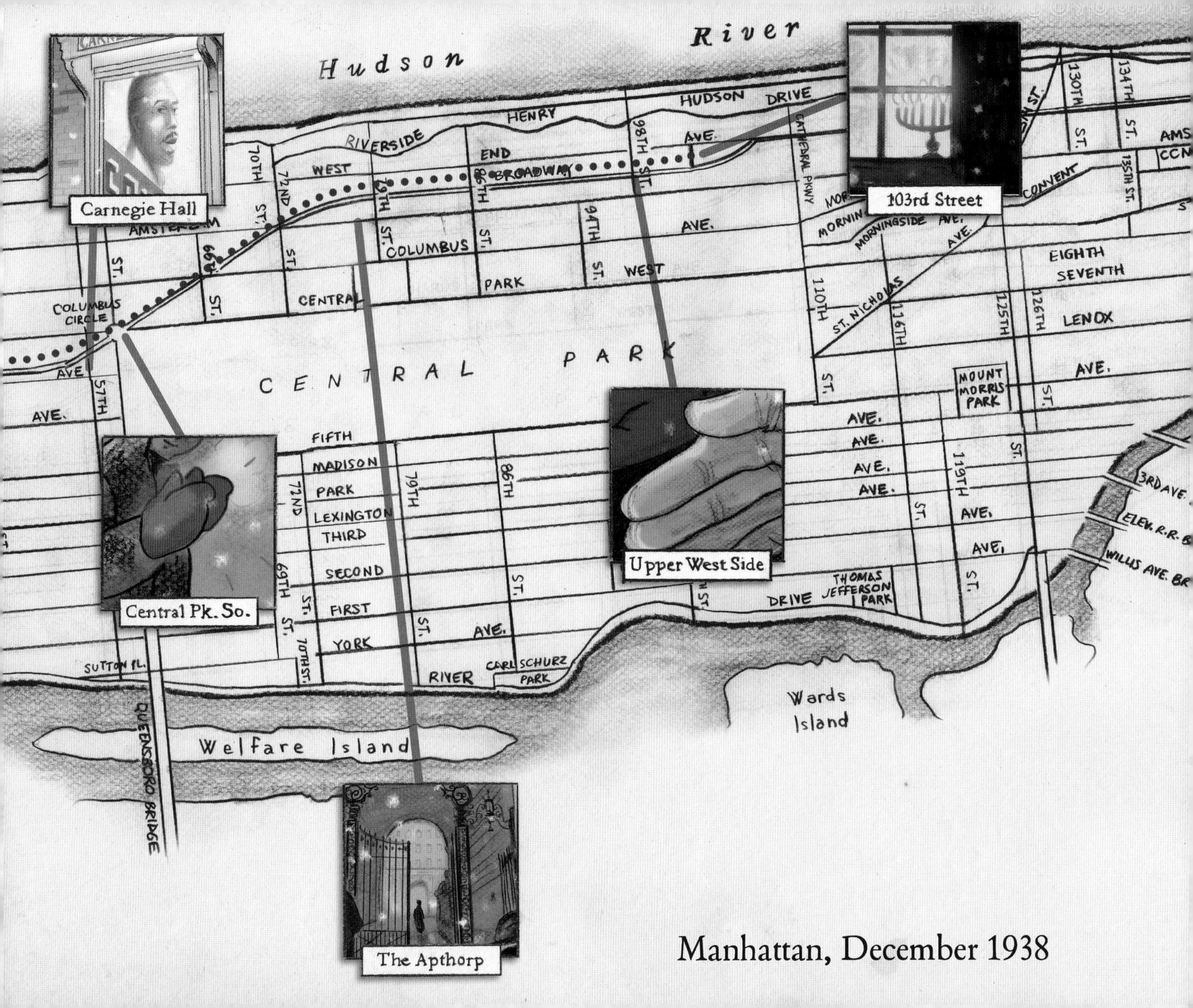

Manhattan, December 1938

For Viviana Mireille Simon —R.S and T.S.
For my steady, steadfast Siena —M.S.

Together we would like to thank the generous and eagle-eyed readings of our dear family and friends: Hildegard McKinnon, Viviana Mireille Simon, Siena Siegel, Clio Siegel, Julien Siegel, Marie-Claire & Edward Siegel, Gene Yang, Devin McIntyre, Lauren Wohl, Ian Lendler, Jason Eaton, Neal Porter, Ayana Byrd, Karen Hopenwasser, Ellen Cowhey, Oya Inal, Wendy Lukehart, Ben Hatke, Karina Edwards, Hilary Sycamore, Eben Mears, Kimmy Ng, Jill Gilbert, John Canemaker, John Sargent, Jon Yaged, and the whole Roaring Brook team—Andrew Arnold, Anne Diebel, Jill Freshney, Allene Cassagnol, and Simon Boughton.

Published by Roaring Brook Press
Roaring Brook Press is a division of Holtzbrinck Publishing Holdings Limited Partnership
175 Fifth Avenue, New York, New York 10010
mackids.com

Library of Congress Cataloging-in-Publication Data
Simon, Richard, 1959–
Oskar and the eight blessings / written by Richard and Tanya Simon ; illustrated by Mark Siegel.
pages cm
Summary: A young Jewish refugee from Nazi Germany arrives in New York City on the seventh night of Hanukkah and receives small acts of kindness while exploring the city.
ISBN 978-1-59643-949-8 (hardback)
[1. Kindness—Fiction. 2. Refugees—Fiction. 3. Jews—Fiction. 4. Holocaust, Jewish (1939–1945)—Fiction. 5. Hanukkah—Fiction.] I. Simon, T. R. (Tanya R.), author. II. Siegel, Mark, 1967– illustrator. III. Title.
PZ7.1.S56Os 2015
[E]–dc23
2015005061

Roaring Brook Press books may be purchased for business or promotional use. For information on bulk purchases please contact Macmillan Corporate and Premium Sales Department at (800) 221-7945 x5442 or by email at specialmarkets@macmillan.com.

First edition 2015
Book design by Mark Siegel and Andrew Arnold
Printed in China by Toppan Leefung Printing Ltd., Dongguan City, Guangdong Province

1 3 5 7 9 10 8 6 4 1 2